Written by April Madres

Co-Written & Illustrated by Ted Irvine

Edited by Ryan Gantz

Photos by Niv Shah

for
santos
and the adventures you will have

she always makes me smile
even if i've been sad for awhile
a true friend each and every day
in my heart is where she'll always stay

around the backyard with me what do i see?

my dog

Out of the blue, they appear
announcing that summer is here
their bellies lit up the night time sky
try to catch them as they fly by

around the backyard with me what do i see?

fireflies

A celebrity amongst his feathered friends
he can be spotted until daytime ends
with his bright red cloak and a voice full of song
in my eyes, he can do no wrong.

around the backyard with me what do i see?

a cardinal

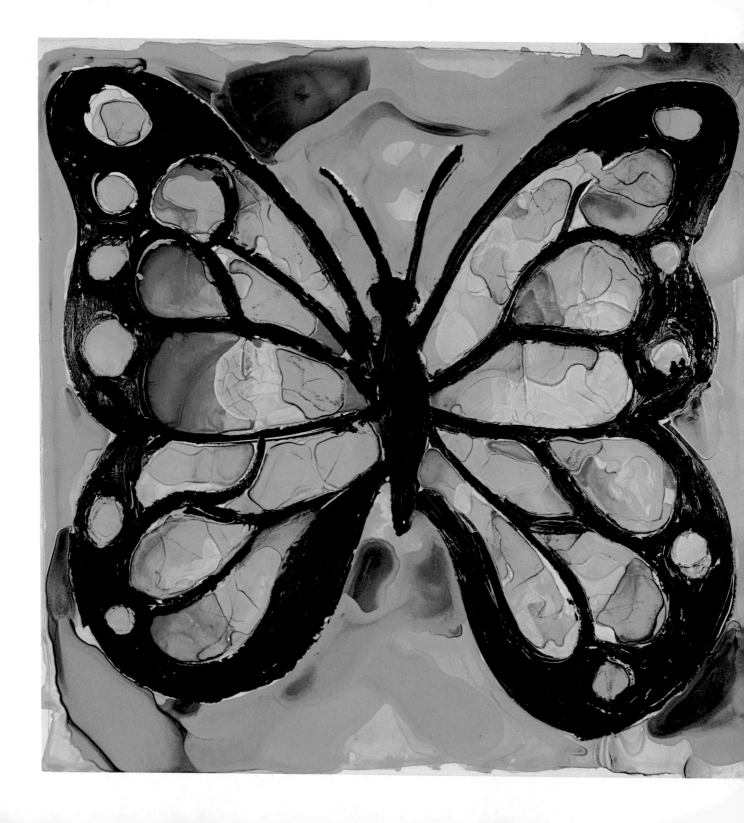

Wings dipped in colorful hues
i loved to follow her as she flew
her time with us is very brief
but she leaves us her kids on a leaf

around the backyard with me what do i see?

a butterfly

always hopping to and fro
in the heat and never in snow
sunning on his lily pad
catching flies makes him glad

around the backyard with me what do i see?

a frog

dotted with freckles just like me
for all the world to enjoy and see
she lands with beauty and with grace
and has the most angelic face

around the backyard with me what do i see?

a ladybug

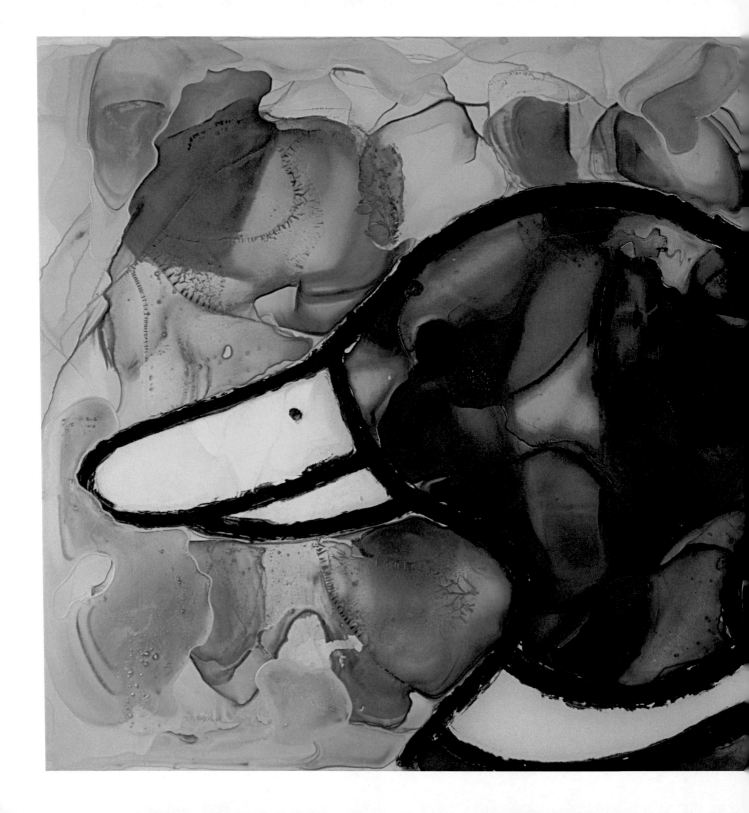

he waddles when he walks
he quacks when he talks
he plunges his head to find some fish
in his mind, they're simply delish

around the backyard with me what do i see?

a duck

under the cover of night
he scavenges for a bite
in his path, he leaves a mess
and causes my parents much distress

around the backyard with me what do i see?

a raccoon

this is a creature i find a bit scary
some of them can even be hairy
she makes a web to catch her prey
sometimes i run into them when i play

around the backyard with me what do i see?

a spider

a winged guardian of the night
seeing mice is when she takes flight
her distinctive voice fills the nighttime air
her majestic beauty is quite rare

around the backyard with me what do i see?

when you hear my buzzing sound
you will know that i am around
if you see me around - i must tell you one thing
you look scary to me and I can pack a nasty sting

around the backyard with me what do i see?

a bee

he's a gluttonous little chap
stealing acorns from my lap
his stuffed cheeks tell me acorns are so yummy
and help to fill up his little round tummy

around the backyard with me what do i see?

a chipmunk

he's got a built in GPS
unfortunately, it leaves a mess
carrying his home on his back
is useful when the beetles attack

around the backyard with me what do i see?

a snail

where she will be
is perched atop a tree
savoring the breezes in the fresh air
guarding her nest with utmost care

around the backyard with me what do i see?

a bluejay

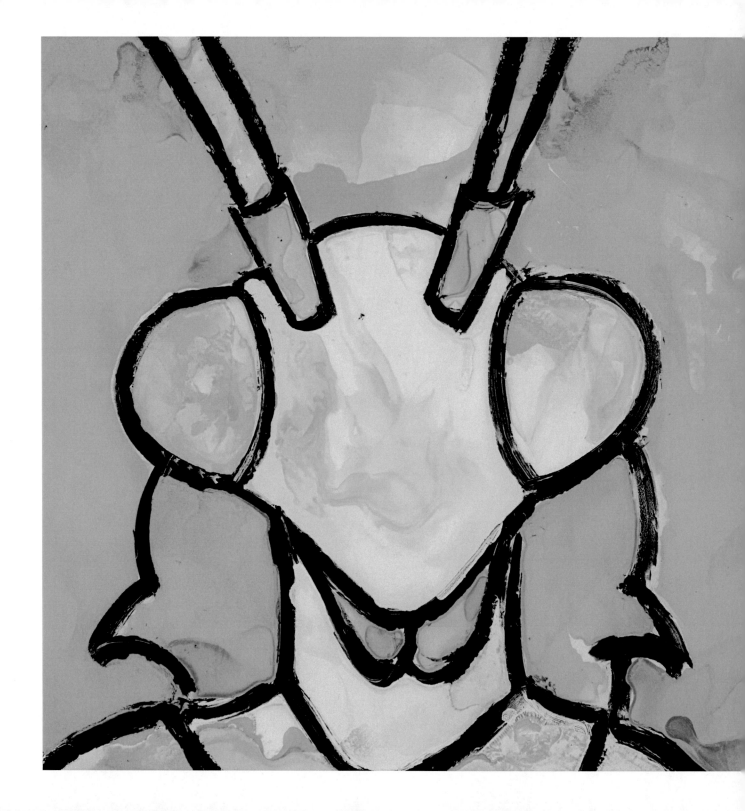

one would think he'd be quite mellow
but he's far from being a religious fellow
spiky legs and big green alien eyes
watch out bugs - you will meet your demise

around the backyard with me what do i see?

a praying mantis

he reminds me of our beloved pooch
but mommy says he can't give me a smooch
sly and quick on his feet
chickens are his favorite treat

around the backyard with me what do i see?

a fox

More Books To Read!

What's Pink?

Teach your kids about all the things that can be pink with the fun call and response rhymes in this book. Vibrant illustrations and beautiful typography bring the couplets to life.

Under the Sea with Me

A fun read to introduce your kids to marine life and the adventures you can have in the ocean.

Under the sea with me, what do I see? A Clownfish!

The Authors

April Madres

April's day time gig is designing web based and instructional led training for the federal government. Outside of work, she spends her cooking, hitting the playgrounds with her kids and squeezing in some runs.

Ted Irvine

When not daydreaming of tropical islands, Ted is the Senior Director of Design at Vox Media. You can usually find him drawing ideas on the glass walls at Vox HQ in DC, all hopped up on caffeine.

Made in the USA
Middletown, DE
04 November 2015